Before reading

Look at the book cover together an ... title. Ask, "What do you think will h ... ?"

Level 12 provides furt ... **'s** introduced in this series. Thi ... 'd's reading skills and ... dently.

During

Offer plenty ... child reads the story. Listen carefull ... nts in the text.

All the **Key Word** ... evel 12 have been introduced in earlier stories and ... be familiar. If the child hesitates over a word, practise reading it together. If the word is phonically decodable, you can sound out the letters and blend the sounds to read the word ("d-o-g, dog"). Praise the child for their effort, then return to the story.

Pause every few pages and ask questions to check the child's understanding of what they have read. If they begin to lose concentration, stop reading and save the page for later.

Celebrate the child's achievement and come back to the story the next day.

After reading

After reading this book, ask, "Did you enjoy the story? What did you like about it?" Encourage the child to share their opinions.

Use the comprehension questions on page 54 to check the child's understanding and recall of the text.

Ladybird

Series Consultant: Professor David Waugh
With thanks to Kulwinder Maude

LADYBIRD BOOKS

UK | USA | Canada | Ireland | Australia
India | New Zealand | South Africa

Ladybird Books is part of the Penguin Random House group of companies whose addresses can be found at global.penguinrandomhouse.com.
www.penguin.co.uk www.puffin.co.uk www.ladybird.co.uk

Penguin Random House UK

Original edition of Key Words with Peter and Jane first published by Ladybird Books Ltd 1964
Series updated 2023
This book first published 2023
001

Illustrations by Pablo Gallego with colour work by Valeria Abatzoglu
Based on characters and design by Gustavo Mazali

With thanks to Liz Pemberton for her contributions in advising on the illustrations
With thanks to Inclusive Minds for connecting us with their Inclusion Ambassador network, and in particular thanks to Guntaas Kaur Chugh for her input on the illustrations

Printed in China

The authorized representative in the EEA is Penguin Random House Ireland, Morrison Chambers, 32 Nassau Street, Dublin D02 YH68

A CIP catalogue record for this book is available from the British Library

ISBN: 978-0-241-51108-4

All correspondence to:
Ladybird Books
Penguin Random House Children's
One Embassy Gardens, 8 Viaduct Gardens, London SW11 7BW

MIX
Paper from responsible sources
FSC® C018179
FSC www.fsc.org

Key Words

with Peter and Jane

12c

The street party

Based on the original
Key Words with Peter and Jane
reading scheme and research by William Murray

Original edition written by William Murray
This edition written by Swapna Haddow
Illustrated by Pablo Gallego with colour work by Valeria Abatzoglu
Based on characters and design by Gustavo Mazali

Peter rushed downstairs. He could hear people chatting in the hallway.

It was the Grant family from next door.

Amber and Will had come over to finish their outfits for the street party that afternoon. They were going to help Peter and Jane with their outfits too.

Keen to get started, the children chatted happily. Then, Mr Grant cleared his throat. "Listen, everyone," he said. "I have bad news."

"I've just found out that the street party this afternoon isn't going to happen," Mr Grant said.

Peter's mouth dropped in surprise.

"What?" Jane cried. "Why?"

Mr Grant shook his head sadly and said, "There's going to be a rainstorm later this afternoon."

Everyone walked out of the front door, and the children looked up at the blue sky.

"I know the sun is out now," Mrs Grant said. "But there will be lots of rain this afternoon."

It didn't look like the blue sky would turn into dark storm clouds and rain, but the children knew that Mr and Mrs Grant were right.

"The people who were bringing the food have said they won't come because of the storm," Mrs Grant went on.

"Oh no!" Peter cried. He had wanted to try all the food.

Mum squeezed his hand. "It wouldn't be safe for them to set up their food tents in the rain," she said.

"The band has pulled out too," Dad said.

"No! This is so sad," Will said.

"I wanted to put on my bright outfit!" Amber cried.

"You can still put it on, if you like," Mum told her with a smile. "It won't be for the street party, but I'd love to see it."

"Thank you, but I wanted everyone to see it," Amber said. "Mum and I worked so hard on it."

Peter could see Amber's outfit through her bag. The outfit was yellow, and there were shimmering jewels on it.

Peter, Jane and Mum headed into the living room with the Grant family. Dad went to the kitchen to make hot drinks for everyone, thinking that might help them all feel better.

"Would you like to play a game?" Peter asked Amber.

"Not really," Amber said. She looked down at her outfit bag.

Jane saw how sad Amber was, and she put her arm round her. "I wish there was something we could do," Jane said.

"Mum, could we still have the street party in the rain?" Peter asked.

Mum shrugged. "We could, but with no food or music, it wouldn't be much of a party," she said.

By the time Dad came in with the hot drinks, no one in the room was speaking. They were all very sad. Everyone was thinking about how much fun the street party would have been.

"I wish we could set up our own street party," Amber said, then she sighed.

"That would be fun," Peter said.

"Maybe we could have a party in our house," Jane said. "That way, we can dress up in the outfits that we worked so hard on."

"Dad and I could make some food," Mum said, thinking hard. "We have burgers in the freezer."

"We have some crisps and dips in our house," Mrs Grant added. "We could bring them over."

Amber looked happier. "What if every house on the street had a party?" she said. "Then, it would be a little bit like a street party."

"Yes, Amber!" cried Will. "Mum and Dad could be the band and play music in the street. Everyone will hear the music through their windows!"

"I wouldn't mind playing," Mrs Grant said, grinning at Mr Grant.

"But where could we shelter from the rain while we play?" Mr Grant asked.

"We have a big tent you could use," Mum said. "We could set it up outside the house for you."

"That's a good idea!" Mr Grant said, looking pleased.

"I wish we had a tent that could cover the street," Jane said. "Then we wouldn't have to stay in our houses. We could see everyone's outfits and eat outdoors."

"I think you might be on to something there, Jane," Mum said. "We have a very big waterproof sheet somewhere. We could string it up on the trees in the street and make a shelter for everyone."

"Maybe we can have the street party after all!" Amber cried.

The clouds in the sky were getting very dark.

"Let's speak to people in the street. We need to pull this party together quickly," Dad said.

Mr and Mrs Grant headed next door to get their musical instruments, and Mum went to find the big waterproof sheet.

Dad went over the street to speak to the Shahs, while the children looked at Amber's party outfit in the living room.

"Oh, Amber! This is fantastic," Jane said. She ran her hands over Amber's outfit.

Amber grinned. "Mum and I made it last year for a float at the carnival," she said. "We made outfits with some other children."

"That must have been so much fun," Jane said.

"Dad, Maya and I cheered them on as their float went past," Will said. "There was lots of music and good food."

"You should come with us next time," Amber said to Peter and Jane.

"We would love to," Jane said, and Peter nodded.

Dad came home to get the waterproof sheet.

The Shahs thought that it was a great idea to still have the party! They had asked if everyone could bring out chairs and tables so that the people who lived on the street could all sit and eat their food side by side.

"We could all bring something to eat," Mrs Shah had said to Dad.

Peter and Jane couldn't wait to eat Mrs Shah's food. They loved her cooking.

While Mum and Dad helped to set up their tent, lots of people came out of their houses to see what was going on.

"We have a waterproof sheet too," one person said.

"And so do we," another added.

Dad thanked everyone. "Now that we have so many sheets, we can cover the street!" he said, laughing. "This is going to be the best street party ever."

Suddenly, there was a clap of thunder overhead. People rushed to string the waterproof sheets from tree to tree. Soon, the street looked like one big tent.

People found chairs and tables from their homes and placed them under the shelter of the big sheets. The tables and chairs were all very different, but somehow that made the street party even more fantastic.

Mrs Shah and Sana found some strings of lights, and Peter and Jane helped to put them up under the big sheets. Now, the shelter glowed with pretty lights.

"It's like being under a starry sky!" Jane said.

Mum found some lamps to use for light as well.

At last, the shelter was lit up, and not a second too soon. The sky was now very dark.

The first drops of rain pounded hard on the sheets. Everyone stopped to see just how waterproof the street-party shelter really was.

"It works!" Dad said, and everyone in the shelter cheered.

"It's time for us to put on our party outfits," Jane said.

As the adults found food for lunch, the children went into their houses and got dressed for the party.

Jane and Will had made their party outfits together. They were sheep!

They had painted boxes and used cotton wool balls to make the sheep's fluffy wool. Every time they walked, they left trails of cotton wool.

Maya was a sunflower, and Peter was a fox. Peter sat down by a big bowl of Mrs Shah's curry.

"I think Jane and Will have been here," Peter said. Big spoonfuls of the curry had been eaten, and he spotted cotton wool balls on the seats.

There were fairies, animals, flowers and wizards, but everyone thought that Amber's stunning outfit was the best.

"I like your bear outfit!" Jane said to a girl she hadn't chatted to before.

"Thank you," the girl said.

"Do you live on this street?" Jane asked. "Which house is yours?"

"That one over there," said the girl, pointing to a house just a few doors down from Peter and Jane's house.

1st

Jane and the little girl weren't the only people to make new friends that day. Everyone laughed and had fun, and many people chatted with old friends and made new ones.

Mr and Mrs Grant played music all afternoon as the rain poured. Soon, lots of people were on their feet, moving to the music. They had a fantastic time.

When Mr and Mrs Grant stopped playing their music to have some food, Will played his keyboard. Mum, Dad and Mr Grant had helped him bring the keyboard out of the house, and Amber sang along while her brother played.

"The Grants are a very talented family," Mrs Shah said to Peter and Mum.

"They are!" Mum said.

Later that afternoon, the rain slowed. Then, the dark clouds blew away, and at last the rain stopped.

Soon, the sun came out, and Dad thought it was time to take down the shelter.

Most people went back inside their houses as Dad and a few others tipped the rain off the waterproof sheets. The rainwater splashed down on to the street and into the drains.

When all the rain had been tipped off, Dad started to take the sheets down, but one sheet still had a lot of rainwater on it.

Suddenly, as Dad started to fold up the sheet, the water tipped over his head!

“At least Will’s keyboard isn’t wet!” Mum laughed, as she rushed out to Dad with some towels.

After the street shelter had been taken down, everyone sat round the long table. Then, the Grants started to play music again. Soon, all of the people at the street party had formed a line.

The conga line went on for so long that Mr Shah’s back started to hurt, but he didn’t want to stop!

At last, Mr Shah sat down in a chair at the table, where many others soon joined him to chat happily about the fantastic street party.

“I think it’s time for ice cream,” Mum said, clapping her hands.

“Great idea!” said Jane. She jumped up to help Mum, dropping cotton wool balls everywhere she went. Other people got some tubs of ice cream from inside their houses.

Jane and Sana Shah scooped ice creams for all the children.

Amber, Maya and Peter all picked banana ice cream, then they found a sunny spot on the street where they could sit down. Will joined them with a scoop of raspberry ice cream, and Jane and Sana soon came along too, with scoops of mint and some new friends.

"This is the best street party I've ever been to," Peter said.

The other children all thought it was too.

"I can't wait for next year's party," Jane said.

"Fingers crossed for rain!" said Peter.

Questions

Answer these questions about the story.

1 Why isn't the street party going to happen?

2 What does Amber want to wear to the street party?

3 What do people hang up over the street to make a shelter?

4 Why are there cotton wool balls all over the place?

5 Who plays music at the party?

6 Why do you think Peter wants it to rain at next year's street party?